ANNA BANANA AND ME

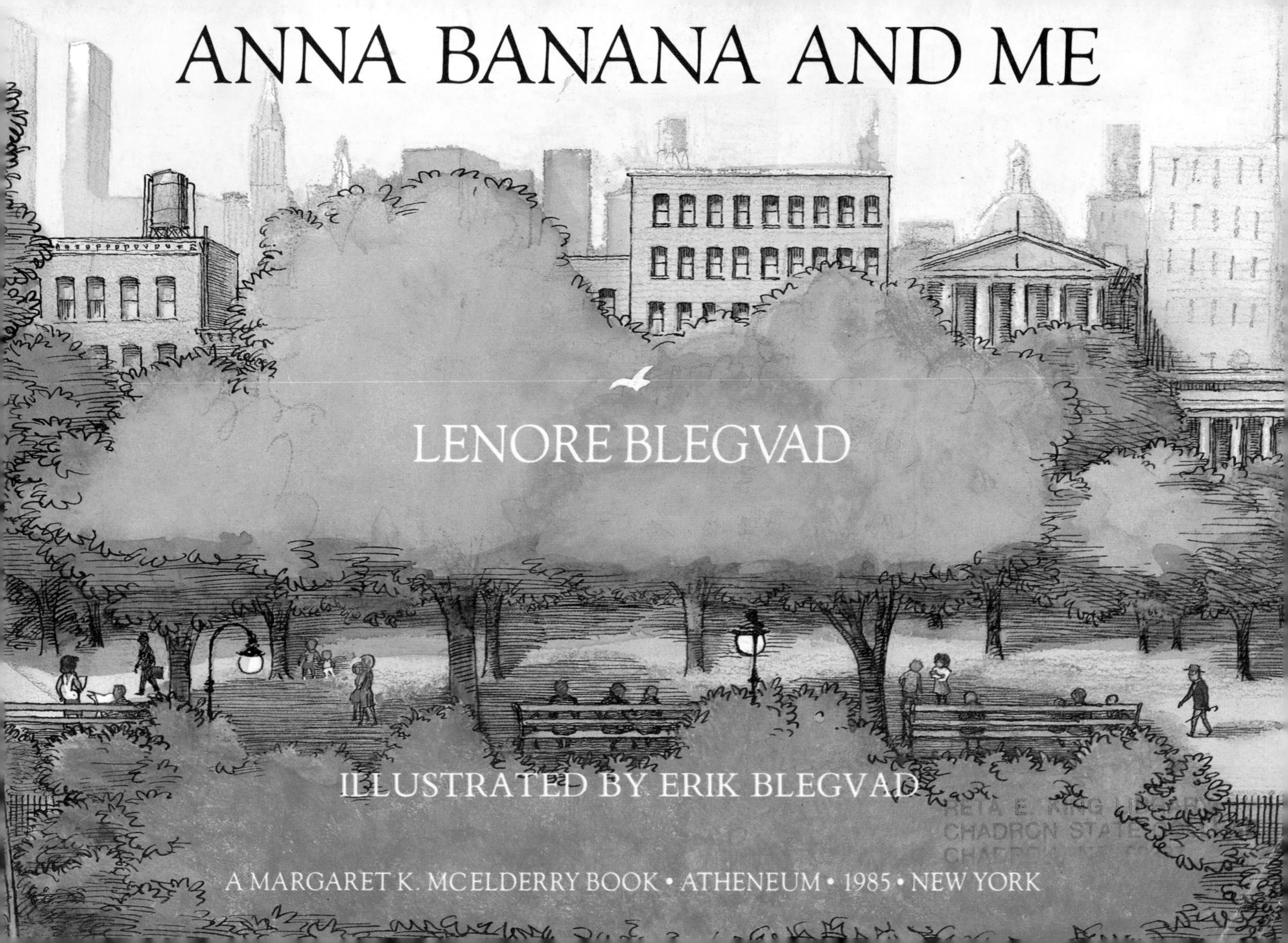

ANNA BANANA AND ME

LENORE BLEGVAD

ILLUSTRATED BY ERIK BLEGVAD

A MARGARET K. MCELDERRY BOOK • ATHENEUM • 1985 • NEW YORK

Library of Congress Cataloging in Publication Data

Blegvad, Lenore.
Anna Banana and me.

"A Margaret K. McElderry book."
Summary: Anna Banana's fearlessness inspires a
playmate to face his own fears.
[1. Fear—Fiction] I. Blegvad, Erik, ill.
II. Title.
PZ7.B618My 1985 [E] 84-457
ISBN 0-689-50274-5

Published simultaneously in Canada by McClelland & Stewart, Ltd.
Printed in Hong Kong by the South China Printing Company
First Edition

In memory of my mother
who named her

On the steps, in the park, stands Anna Banana.
"Come on!" she calls. "Follow me!"
and she runs.

I run too—
past the fountain, past the statue, to a place where
branches hang low.
We crawl underneath, away from the sun,
into the shadows behind wooden benches.

Inside, the earth feels cold.
There are dead leaves and pebbles.
A white pigeon's feather shines from a twig.
It's a place no one has ever been. Or seen.
Dark and hidden.

Something scuffles through the leaves,
scratch, *scratch*, *scratch*.
Feet walk by out in the sun.
"A feather is magic!" whispers Anna Banana.
She grabs it from the branch.

Then, “Come on,” she says.
We crawl out into the light.
Anna Banana stands up. She has leaves in her hair.
“Bye!” she says.
She waves at me
and she is gone.
So I go home.

Some other day, on my street, I meet Anna Banana.
"Is this where you live?" she asks.

I watch her do a dance in my hall.
And in the dusty mirror another Anna Banana dances with her.

A white staircase reaches up to the dark.
"Come on," says Anna Banana.
We climb many stairs, to a hall full of
shadows, where I never go.

Behind rows of doors are people I never see.
“Whooo-wheee!” calls Anna Banana into the shadows.
“Whooo-wheee!” her voice comes back.
Anna Banana laughs.
“Hello, echo!” she says.

Down the white stairs
Anna Banana runs on ahead,
faster and faster,
galloping down.
I see her hand slide on the bannister.

Then, “Bye!” she calls up to me.
And “Bye!” comes the echo.
The street door slams.
I go home, up the stairs.

In the playground, on a swing, sits Anna Banana.
"Push me!" she calls.
And I push her, high.
"Higher!" she says.

She flies up and back,
up and back,
higher than high.
"I'm over the treetops," calls Anna Banana.
It makes me dizzy to watch her.

The sand in the sandbox is cool and damp.
"We'll have a party," says Anna Banana.
"Let's pretend it's your birthday,
and I'll be the baker."
She makes me a cake,

with ice-cream-stick candles.
I take a deep breath and blow them all out.
“What did you wish for?” asks Anna Banana.
But I didn’t wish.
I always forget.

We make castles and roads.
My castle is biggest.
But Anna Banana's has a moat and a turret.
When hers is finished, she smashes it flat.

She brushes sand from her hands.
Then “Bye!” she says and skips out of the playground.
I put a leaf flag on my castle before I go home.

In the park, on the statue, sits Anna Banana.
“Come on up!” she shouts.
I climb up and we sit on the statue’s lap.
We pretend to read from his big stone book.

"Once upon a time," reads Anna Banana, "there was a horrible goblin!"
Above us a pigeon sits on the statue's hat.
I look up at him,
and he blinks down at me.
Anna Banana goes on reading.
She likes goblin stories.
I don't.

"And the goblin was as big as this whole statue!"
reads Anna Banana.
"And he had a horrible, red, enormous face!
Like a great big tomato,
with great big red ears that stuck out like this!"
Anna Banana spreads her arms wide.
I hold onto the statue's hand.

Anna Banana stops reading and slides off the
statue's lap.
She stands on one of his stone shoes and looks across
the park.

Suddenly she shouts, "Watch out! Watch out! The tomato face is coming!"
I shut my eyes tight.
The tomato face is coming!
And Anna Banana is laughing!
I hear her jump down to the ground.
"Bye!" I hear her call.
And then she is gone.

But I am still here.
I can't go anywhere.
The tomato face is coming!
I can't move,
or open my eyes.
I can only hold onto the statue's hand.
Anna Banana can laugh.
She isn't afraid.
But I am.
I'm not Anna Banana.

Oh! What's that?!
Something soft has touched my hand!
Is it the goblin? What shall I do?
I open my eyes and take a peek.
It is only a feather from the pigeon above.
A feather?
"A feather is magic!" said Anna Banana.
I snatch it up and remember to wish.

And right away, I can open my eyes!
I can jump down from the statue!
I can laugh at the goblin!
I'm just as brave as Anna Banana!

“Bye, pigeon!” I call.
He flies up to the treetops.
And I run all the way home.